DISCARD

Spaghetti

is NOT a Finger Food
(and other life lessons)

Written by Jodi Carmichael
Illustrated by Sarah Ackerley

Little Pickle Press

To my daughters, Sarah Grace and Emma MacKenzie,
your imaginations inspire me. To my husband, Drew, your
belief in me keeps me writing. To my parents, your
encouragement helped me follow my dreams.
~ J.C.

For my awesome brothers, Alex and Corey, and for my
wonderful parents who would do it all over again.
~ S.A.

Library of Congress Cataloging-in-Publication Data is available.
Library of Congress Catalog Card Number 2012952445

ISBN 978-0-9829938-8-0

16 15 14 13 12   1 2 3 4 5 6 7 8 9 10

Little Pickle Press, Inc.
3701 Sacramento Street #494
San Francisco, CA 94118

Please visit us at www.littlepicklepress.com.

Table of Contents

Lesson 1

Mrs. Winters Does Not Like to Be Interrupted

(Even if it is a life or death emergency)

I'm having a few issues at school. My teacher, Mrs. Winters, and I don't see eye to eye. To Mrs. Winters and my mom that means that when Mrs. Winters talks I don't always listen very well. I think sometimes she doesn't listen very well when I'm talking. I don't say that, though. That would be Very Bad Manners on my part.

Just this morning I tried to tell her that the class gecko, T-Rex, was stuck in the radiator, but she said "Not To Interrupt Her For The Fourth Time This Morning!" She seemed kind of screechy so I said, in my most patient and calming voice, "When I get upset it helps me to calm down by taking three deep breaths."

Then I had to take a time out in the hall.

There wasn't much to do out there, so I conducted an experiment. I wondered how many times I could spin in a circle before I puked. I was up to 24 when a sixth grader walked by and called me a "weirdo." I stopped spinning and immediately smashed into the wall. Apparently, he found this very funny, because he laughed until he snorted.

Animal Habitats
   rainforest
   wetlands
   desert
   marine
   arctic
   grasslands

Reports due Tue

"At least I don't snort!" I called in his general direction.

It was actually kind of hard to focus because my head was spinning so fast I had to squeeze my eyes shut. My stomach started to get squeegy. I think I had gotten pretty close to puking! Awesome!

Lesson 2

Gecko Facts

1. Geckos weren't dinosaurs

2. Some Geckos like heat

3. Geckos are NOT Bar-B-Que

Girls Are Confusing

(Geckos aren't for everyone)

Luckily, while I was taking some time to think about my behavior and testing out my theories on spinning and puking, Mrs. Winters found T-Rex before he got too toasty.

I rushed across our classroom, through Jack and Evan's science project volcano, to Mrs. Winters. I had about a thousand facts about geckos jumping around in my head that I was sure she would love to know.

"Mrs. Winters, Mrs. Winters," I called as those facts started spilling out of my mouth.

I squeezed in front of the other kids who were crowded around Mrs. Winters and T-Rex.

"Did you know that although geckos are often mistaken for descendants of dinosaurs they really aren't, but birds are? And did you know

that Leopard Geckos like T-Rex are found in hot countries like India? So T-Rex would prefer to be warm and it is pretty cold out today. I believe that's why he was curled up in the radiator. He was listening to his natural instincts! But, Mrs. Winters," I said, "Geckos don't like to be barbecued in elementary schools."

Mackenzie and Grace laughed. That surprised me.

"Do you think T-Rex being fried is funny?" I asked them.

They laughed even more. Mackenzie rolled her eyes.

"Connor, you need . . ." Mrs. Winters began.

I interrupted her because I thought maybe Mackenzie and Grace didn't believe me.

"Although it seems very obvious to me that a gecko wouldn't want to be cooked at school, I could Google it for you . . . just to make sure," I said.

I was quite sure they'd appreciate my fact-finding methods and who wouldn't want to know more about geckos?

"Whatever," they said at the same time.

That made them laugh even harder and they walked back to their desks.

"Girls," I muttered.

"Connor, you need to settle down and get back to work," said Mrs. Winters.

"But, I have more to tell you about geckos," I said.

Mrs. Winters' face got all wrinkly, especially between her eyes. She took in a large gulp of air. She held it for a long time. I started counting the seconds, but I lost track when I got to six. That's when I started thinking about the spaghetti we were having for lunch.

"I hope there are meatballs," I said to Mrs. Winters.

Mrs. Winters' big gulp of air whooshed out in a long deep sigh.

"Just go sit down, Connor. Please," she said.

At least she didn't sound screechy anymore.

Lesson 3

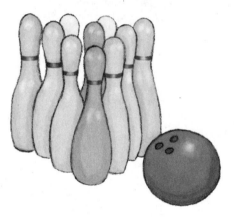

Mr. O'Brien Does Not Believe Rules Are to Be Broken—Ever

(Plastic bowling pins are a
lot harder than they look)

Mr. O'Brien and I don't play by the same rules. He

tells me that almost every gym class. I think this

is some sort of joke and he's trying to be funny.

He laughs every time he says it, even though he's

said it since I was in kindergarten.

Today we are playing with the indoor bowling

set. Mr. O'Brien started explaining how everything

was going to work. I listened a long time. But

then, I started thinking about how the pins looked

a lot like miniature baseball bats. I wondered what was invented first: bowling or baseball?

Mr. O'Brien set up the teams and I was with Jack and Evan. They're nicer to me than some of the other boys, so I was happy to be with them. They didn't seem to be too happy about me playing with them, though. They kept muttering about how I had wrecked their volcano when I rushed to save T-Rex. The life of a real live gecko is more important than a slightly smushed fake volcano. That seemed pretty obvious to me, so I ignored them and began setting up the pins.

"Hey, Connor, what are you doing?" Evan asked me.

I ignored him and kept setting up the pins.

"Hey, Connor! What are you doing?" Evan asked louder.

This time I looked at him. I wondered if he was kidding around. I figured he must have been, because he could see I was setting up the pins.

"Are you deaf, Connor? Mr. O'Brien said the girls are setting up the pins!" Evan said.

He yelled right in my ear.

That really hurt, so I swung a bowling pin around and smacked him on the head. It made a deep thudding sound which I didn't

expect. I thought it would sound more like that dinging sound you hear in cartoons. Evan grabbed his head and started crying.

That's when Mr. O'Brien said it again.

"Well, Connor, it seems like we don't play by the same rules."

"Mr. O'Brien, did you know that a joke is only funny the first time you tell it?" I asked him.

I wondered why no one had told him this.

Mr. O'Brien's face went Twizzler red and his voice went all deep and rumbly. He pointed to the door.

"Connor, to the office!" he said.

Lesson 4

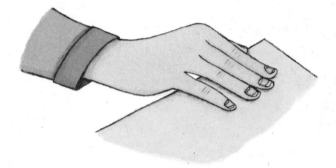

Smooth Things Are Calming

(Ms. Robinson needs a manicure)

When I got to the principal's office I rushed to my favorite blue vinyl chair. I like to count how many times I can run my fingers over the seat, next to my legs, before Principal Hoover calls me.

I strongly dislike the red chair that sits across from the blue one. It's old, scratchy, and torn in a few places. It's impossible to sit still in that chair. True story.

One time, I told Ms. Robinson how the cool

smoothness of the blue chair made my body quiet down. She just looked at me and said, "Well, that makes sense, Connor." I thought maybe she was teasing me, but she didn't laugh so that was a good clue that she understood what I meant.

I like Ms. Robinson. She has smooth brown hair like mine, but hers is way longer. Today she had it swooped up on top of her head with a flower pin in it. I like smooth hair best because it doesn't look all wiggly and jumbled like curly hair. I like smooth things because they are easier to look at and they don't make me feel all shaky inside.

Today Ms. Robinson was on the phone when I

sat down. She was telling someone about a stray dog that kept roaming around the school yard. Apparently, it would come right up to the school doors but would shy away if anyone got too close. A stray dog? That reminded me of my old sitter's dog, Charlie. Bonnie and Charlie used to meet me after school every day and I would walk him back to Bonnie's house. It was my favorite part of the day. Bonnie and Charlie used to live just two doors down, but they moved to a farm outside the city. I miss Charlie so much, but my mom said he will love the farm, and Bonnie said we can visit whenever we want. Then Bonnie called us a few weeks ago because Charlie had run away the day after they moved. Now, Charlie is lost.

Was this dog a runaway, too? I wondered what breed. If only I had my *All about Dogs* book with me. I could ask Ms. Robinson some questions and look in my book to match it to a breed. Maybe I could make a sketch - like a missing person's drawing. I could be a dog-finding detective! I had to know more. Did it have dog tags? Did it look vicious?

"Ms. Robinson," I said, "Did you . . ." I didn't get to finish because she shushed me with her hands.

That's when I noticed her finger nails. I fell back into my seat. What a shocker! Ms. Robinson's nails weren't smooth and painted like my Mom's

were. They were rough and jagged and too hard to look at. Ms. Robinson's nails were a Big Disappointment.

I ran my fingers over my seat so fast that I counted all the way to 314 before Mr. Hoover called me into his office. Finally!

"Wow! You sure are eager today, Connor," said

Mr. Hoover as I sped past him into his neat and tidy office.

He closed the door so we could discuss my Discouraging Day.

"Ms. Robinson should take better care of her nails," I said.

"Oh," said Mr. Hoover, "Why is that?"

"They don't match," I said.

Mr. Hoover's face got all wrinkly and he tilted his head a bit.

"I am confused, Connor. What don't Ms. Robinson's nails match?" he asked.

"They don't match the rest of her. She is so nice and smooth everywhere else and then her nails are completely wrong," I said.

Sometimes it's tiring having to explain myself.

I could feel my face growing hotter and I was getting that jittery feeling in my stomach. I knew pretty soon my arms would get all shaky. I didn't want to get Ms. Robinson into trouble, but those nails were all wrong. I hoped my insides would quiet down if I could make Mr. Hoover understand.

"Couldn't you make her smooth out her nails?" I asked.

Mr. Hoover shook his head and sat down on one of the two large brown leather chairs that sat in front of his desk.

"Listen, Connor, it's none of our business how Ms. Robinson keeps her nails. I can't change Ms. Robinson. But I can talk to Mrs. Rosetti and the two of you can think of some ways for you not to focus on her nails, since they bother you so much."

Mr. Hoover is getting better at talking to me. He doesn't make me feel silly or weird and he doesn't tell me my feelings are wrong. Ever since I started spending more time with Mrs. Rosetti, our resource teacher, I've seen a Big Improvement in Mr. Hoover's attitude toward me. That means he doesn't yell so much.

Last year, in grade two, he did a lot of yelling. He said he wasn't yelling, he was just talking loudly. It sure seemed like yelling to me.

"I like your new voice, Mr. Hoover," I said.

Mrs. Rosetti says it's important to let people know when their behavior has improved so that they know that their hard work is paying off.

"My new voice . . ." began Mr. Hoover.

The lunch bell rang and I sprang from my chair! Spaghetti Monday. My favorite!

"Now, Connor, you'll have to discuss this further with Mrs. Rosetti," Mr. Hoover said as he swooshed me out of his office.

"Okay, Mr. Hoover. Did you know that bowling pins make a loud thudding sound when you smack them against Evan?" I asked.

Mr. Hoover muttered something like, "Oh, brother" or "Oh, bother." It was hard for me to hear him because his hand was in front of his mouth and his voice was all muffled. His shoulders began to twitch and he coughed. The same thing happens to my dad all the time. I used to think he was laughing at me but my dad said it's just hay fever.

"Off to lunch," Mr. Hoover said and swiveled me toward the lunchroom.

I think Mr. Hoover may have hay fever, too. I'll have to remember to ask him about that tomorrow.

Lesson 5

Lunch Time Can Be Tricky

(Spaghetti should never be
eaten with your hands)

I fast-walked to the lunchroom so I could get my
favorite spot right next to the door. If I was late
then I might have to sit in an Unknown Spot like
close to the food line or even worse . . . at the
back of the room in the corner.

I like to be by the door so in case of fire I
would be the first one out. I always make sure I
know where my exits are. Strangely, not everyone
wants to know. In grade one, I always called out

the exits whenever we went to gym or music, but my teacher asked me to stop. She said it was making some of the kids scared because it made

(Just in case)

them worried about fires. I've thought about that a lot. It still doesn't make much sense to me.

The smell of tomatoes and cheese made my stomach gurgle as I turned the corner into the lunchroom. I darted to my spot, relieved to find that no one had taken my chair.

Lunch always goes better for me when I don't need to focus on fire exits.

I dropped my backpack on the chair and stood in line behind a fifth grader named Jessie. She has straight black hair that sits perfectly on her shoulders—not one hair bent or scrunched. I could feel a warm calmness fill my body and slip down my legs and arms. I was sure this was going to be a good lunch!

When I got back to my spot with my tray, Grace and Mackenzie were sitting at my table. I eased into my seat, careful not to let my spaghetti slide off my plate. Last Monday my spaghetti landed on the floor and I had to beg Mrs. Chang for more.

She kept muttering that she "hadn't gone to college for four years to be mopping up spaghetti off the floor."

I told her, "It's okay to be a slow learner, Mrs. Chang. We can't all be good at everything, but four years does seem a long time to learn how to mop."

She just pointed to the food line and said, "Go."

Sluuuurrrrrp!

I was determined not to cross Mrs. Chang today, so I was extra careful.

It all started so well, too. I was eating my spaghetti when a super-long noodle slithered down my chin and slapped me on my neck.

Grace saw this and started to giggle. Mackenzie's eyes got wide as she smiled at me.

"Whoa . . . what a mess!" Mackenzie said.

I've noticed that Mackenzie doesn't smile much unless she's really happy, so I figured she wasn't teasing me.

When I smiled back at her another slippery noodle squeezed out of my mouth and plopped onto my plate. This made Mackenzie laugh. Then her spaghetti squeezed out of her mouth too!

She looked like a wild cavewoman with that spaghetti sauce dripping down her chin! I piled a bunch more spaghetti onto my fork and shoveled it into my mouth. This time both girls laughed so I grabbed more spaghetti with both hands and stuffed it into my mouth. The warm tomato sauce dripped down my arms and actually felt kind of nice. I took a big gulp and that spaghetti slid down my throat.

"Hey, look at me," I grunted and I did my best caveman impression, "Ooga Booga!"

Suddenly the girls stopped laughing and the entire room hushed up. Wow! Everyone was looking at me.

I stood up on my chair and dumped what was left of my spaghetti over my head and shouted, "Me caveman . . . me love spaghetti!"

I could hear snickers and giggles ripple through the room. They thought I was funny!

"Connor James Campbell, spaghetti is not to be eaten with your hands—ever!" Mrs. Chang's

voice rang out from somewhere behind me.

"Oh-oh," I whispered.

I had crossed Mrs. Chang. Rats! I had been so sure that lunch was going to go well today.

They're serving pot roast tomorrow. I think that will turn out better for me, because . . . how much trouble can pot roast be?

Lesson 6

A Library Voice Is Even Quieter Than an Inside Voice

(The newest best book in the universe should never be on the top shelf)

Library is my favorite time of day, even though it's sometimes the hardest time for me.

Today I was almost late because I had to change into my "I♥Dogs" gym t-shirt after my spaghetti incident. But luckily, I zipped into the library right before the bell rang. Unluckily, I was too late to get my favorite spot right next to the computers and the door.

I looked around the room and saw the last

empty seat at the back of the study area. I squished through the blue round tables and plunked into the chair. I tugged out my favorite library books—*Dogs Digest* and *Wild for Dogs* and my own copy of *All about Dogs*. I know almost everything about dogs!

"That's a cool book," said Adam, who was sitting next to me.

He was pointing to my *All about Dogs* book.

"It is the best book in the universe! I always carry my *All about Dogs* book with me. Just in case I need to look up a fact," I said.

I could feel warm bubbles filling up my

stomach. I love telling people about dogs, so I continued.

"I know every breed and where in the world they first came from. I also know that the smallest dog on record is a Chihuahua named Dancer. He lives in Florida. And did you know that archaeologists think that greyhounds are ancient Egyptian dogs?" I asked.

"Uh . . . no," said Adam.

"And did you know . . ." I began.

"Connor, you are not using your library voice. Please try to keep your volume down so the other children can get their work done," said our librarian, Mr. Cohen.

Mr. Cohen then flicked the lights off and on. That was our signal to zip our lips and spy our eyes on him.

"Class, today I would like you to continue working on your project. If you need help finding books, I'll be right here at my desk," he said.

Everyone started pulling their library books out of their bags and whispering to each other about their projects.

"I'm doing my project on dogs," I whispered to Adam.

"Oh, yeah," he whispered back.

He opened a library book and flipped through the pages.

"Yup. It's going to be easy because I already know so much about them," I whispered.

"I'm doing my project on airplanes," said Adam. "They are so cool! Did you know that Orville Wright was the first person to fly a plane?"

"Airplanes? That's the worst idea ever! I

strongly dislike planes. They make too much noise, the seats are jam-packed together, and you never get any good snacks, only peanuts or cookies . . . and the cookies taste like cardboard. I went on a plane last summer to see my Grandpa Terry in Florida and my little sister Chloe got sick and threw up all over my mom. My mom said she thought it was a 'total nightmare that was never going to end'," I said to Adam.

He just sat there with his mouth hanging open. I wondered if my story confused him or maybe he couldn't hear my library whisper so I continued a little louder.

"Of course, the nightmare did end because, as

you can see, I'm not on that plane anymore. True story. Anyway, that's why I'd never do my project on airplanes. Plus, dogs are *way* cooler," I said.

"Connor . . . voice and volume please," said Mr. Cohen from his desk.

"Pfff," muttered Adam.

I figured he had a lot of work to do because he turned his back to me and started flipping through his boring old airplane book again.

I got up and returned my books to Mr. Cohen and was heading toward the animal section just behind the computers, when I saw the best book I had ever seen in my entire life! It was propped up on top of the "New to the Library" book shelf

next to a stuffed dachshund that was sitting in a large blue cardboard dog house.

"*More All about Dogs!*" I gasped.

I had to get that book! It would have all the latest facts and it would be perfect for my project.

I darted across the library and whizzed between the computers all the time thinking about that book. What else had they discovered about dogs? Had they found more breeds? Did they know for sure if greyhounds descended from ancient Egyptian dogs?

I guess that's when my right foot got tangled in the wires of Evan's computer. I staggered forward and smashed my elbow into the back of Mackenzie who was sitting at the table next to him.

"Ow!" cried Mackenzie.

"Watch it!" shouted Evan.

"Uh, sorry," I muttered over my shoulder as I untangled my foot.

They really should move those computers before someone gets hurt.

"Children . . . voices and volume," Mr. Cohen called.

I fast-walked to the book shelf. I tried to reach the top shelf by balancing on my tiptoes on the bottom shelf, but I wasn't quite tall enough. I scanned the library to find a stool and spotted Jane sitting on one near the quiet-reading nook.

I zipped over to her, careful not to go near the computers again.

"Jane, you need to move," I said.

"What?" she said, staring up at me.

She blinked her brown eyes; once, twice, three times.

"I need that stool, so you need to move," I explained.

"Well, I am using it so you'll have to find another one," she said.

She flipped her long blond hair over her

shoulder and looked back down at her book. Didn't she realize that the whole purpose of a stool was to stand on it when something was too high to reach? Like the Newest Best Book in the Universe? I could feel a ball of red fire start to simmer in my chest.

"Go get a chair or sit on the couch in the quiet-reading nook," I said.

Maybe she didn't know that stools were not for sitting on.

"I don't feel like it," she said without looking at me.

That's when that ball of red-fire-hotness exploded up my neck and raced across my face.

I sort of remembered Mrs. Rosetti telling me to take three deep breaths when I started getting hot, but I *really* needed that stool!

My dad says hindsight is 20-20. He says that to me all the time. It means that if we could see into the future we wouldn't make the same mistakes. I think for me that meant I should've stood on a chair to get that book.

Lesson 7

Stools Are for Standing on and Chairs Are for Sitting On

(Everybody has unique challenges - even Jane)

I nudged Jane off the stool, scooped it up, and ran back to the "New to the Library" book shelf.

"Phew! It's still there!" I shouted.

I had forgotten to use my library voice, but I was sure even Mr. Cohen would understand how special this book was since he was a librarian and all.

I stood on the stool but I still couldn't reach the book. Then I climbed up the rest of the book shelf. My fingers got sweaty really fast and my hands started slipping off the shelves, so I quickly grabbed for the book.

"Whoa!" I yelled.

Somehow I knocked the book and the entire dog display off the top shelf as I fell backward onto the carpet.

"Oof!" I grunted when the dog house landed on my head.

It didn't hurt as much as when I tobogganed off our garage roof into a huge mound of snow last winter. My Dad had piled it there when he shoveled our drive way. My mom yelled at me and Dad that day. Apparently, huge mountains of snow can be extremely dangerous for seven-year-olds.

"Connor, are you okay?" Mr. Cohen asked.

I peeked out from the door of the dog house to see Mr. Cohen quickly walking my way. Jane was right next to him. She was crying. My mom always cries when I get hurt, so I figured she was worried about me.

"I'm okay," I said. "You don't

have to worry, Jane. I got the book!"

"Oh, Connor," sighed Mr. Cohen as he pulled the dog house off of my head. "We need to have a talk. Both of you please come with me to the quiet-reading nook," he said.

We sat down on the fluffy yellow couch. I tried not to fidget. It was very hard to sit still with the *More All About Dogs* book sitting coolly in my lap.

I loved the smoothness of its glossy cover and the little bumps of the raised letters in the title. They chose a Golden Retriever for the front cover, which was perfect. Golden Retrievers have one of the softest coats of all purebred dogs. It would have been so wrong if they had used a Portuguese Water Dog. Just thinking about all those curls made my stomach squiggle.

That Golden looked almost exactly like Bonnie's dog, Charlie. Except Charlie's fur was more strawberry-blonde colored. I sure miss them. What if Bonnie couldn't find Charlie? I got thinking about Charlie so much I sort of forgot that Mr. Cohen was still talking.

"Connor, are you listening to me?" Mr. Cohen's

voice woke me from my Charlie daydream. "Did you take that stool from Jane?"

"Yes, I needed it to reach the top shelf," I said.

"Did you ask first?" Mr. Cohen asked.

"Of course," I replied. "But she wouldn't get off, so I nudged her out of the way."

"See! I told you!" Jane said and her face went all red and more tears started forming at the corners of her eyes.

"Connor, you know you don't just take things that other people are using," said Mr. Cohen.

He ran a hand through his wiry gray hair and shook his head. His hair then poked out at rough angles. His head was hard to look at.

"Well, Mr. Cohen, maybe Jane needs to learn to sit on chairs. A stool is used to stand on to reach high things. A chair is used to sit on," I said.

I looked just below his chin so I didn't have to stare directly at that jumbled hair.

Mr. Cohen's lips started quivering and he cleared his throat.

"That's not the point Connor. You are not to push your classmates," said Mr. Cohen. "Please say that you're sorry to Jane."

"Sorry, Jane," I said.

I didn't feel sorry at all.

"Connor, what have you learned?" Mr. Cohen asked.

"That if Jane is sitting on a stool, and I need it, I should stand on a chair instead, which is actually good news, because there are only two stools and there are 32 chairs," I replied. "I counted them last week when we watched that movie about proper library etiquette."

"I think you know that's not what I meant, Connor," he said. "We're out of time, so I'll have to talk to Mrs. Winters about this. Both of you can go pack up."

Then the bell rang and I fast-walked to Mr. Cohen's computer and checked out my book.

I wondered what Mr. Cohen was going to say to Mrs. Winters. But more importantly I wondered if he was going to talk to Mrs. Winters about Jane's confusion about stools. That seemed a Very Simple Fact to me, but as Mrs. Rosetti always says, "We all learn differently and have special abilities and unique challenges."

I guess stools are Jane's unique challenge. I wonder what her special ability is.

Lesson 8

Magic
Wrinkle-No-More
6 fl. oz

Even Numbers Rule!

(Only Superheroes have Magical Super Powers)

Mrs. Winters marched me back to the classroom at the front of the line.

"It seems I'll have to keep a special eye on you today, Connor. It's shaping up to be one of your more active days, isn't it?" Mrs. Winters said.

"Well, Mrs. Winters . . ." I began.

I wanted to explain about Jane and the stool and the Newest Best Book in the Universe, but she interrupted me.

"That wasn't a question, Connor," she said.

Her voice was high pitched again, but it wasn't screechy like in the morning. I noticed that Mrs. Winters's face was looking particularly scrunchy now. I knew that when Mrs. Winters's face got that scrunched and wrinkled it meant we weren't seeing eye-to-eye and I needed to be quiet.

I'd just have to wait and tell Mrs. Rosetti when I saw her at 2:30. That was 54 minutes away. Usually, it is hard for me to wait to see her because I always have something important to talk to her about. Today I figured it would be a lot easier to wait, because I was doing my eight-times table when we got back to the classroom.

My legs were feeling extra bouncy just thinking about those even numbers.

I like even numbers way better than odd numbers. You can divide them up into pairs, and no numbers are left over. For example, the number four can have two pairs of two, but the number five has problems. You would have to make two pairs of two and then one number would be on his own, without a buddy. It's no fun without a buddy.

The best thing about math is that it follows set rules that never change. Ever. If two times two equals four today it will equal four tomorrow, too.

The next best thing about math is that I am

$8 \times 5 = 40$

$8 \times 4 = 32$

$8 \times 3 = 24$

$8 \times 6 = 48$

$8 \times 2 = 16$

$8 \times 7 = 56$

$8 \times 8 = 64$

$8 \times 1 = 8$

$8 \times 9 = 72$

very, very good at it. My mom says I am "Gifted in Math." That means it's super easy for me to focus on math problems and I don't get so distracted. When I do math, I never start to think about dogs or dinosaurs or what we're eating for lunch. That means I never get into any trouble when I'm doing math. Not ever. That is a nice break for me.

Last month, when I got my fourth 100 percent on a math test, Mrs. Winters said, "Connor, your brain truly amazes me." True story!

That's when Mrs. Winters started giving me advanced math work.

She made my whole body feel bouncy that day!

My legs were getting bouncier and bouncier

as we walked down the hall. When we passed the kindergarten class, I couldn't keep those times tables inside any more. I started whispering the eight-times table between bounces.

"Eight times one is eight."

BOUNCE

"Eight times two is sixteen."

BOUNCE

"Eight times three is twenty-four."

BOUNCE

I stopped counting at eight times four because I could feel Mrs. Winters staring at me. I knew I was in trouble when she used her slow talking voice.

"And . . ." Mrs. Winters said, "Absolutely . . . No

. . . Bouncing."

That is when I noticed that Mrs. Winters's face was looking completely wrinkled. That reminded me of a TV commercial I had seen. It said that you could buy a special cream that would take away your wrinkles and make you look ten years younger. They guaranteed it or your money refunded.

"Mrs. Winters, you have way more wrinkles than my mom does," I said.

"Pardon me?" Mrs. Winters said.

She stopped walking and crouched down next to me.

"You have way more wrinkles than my mom," I repeated louder this time, so that she could hear me. "*And* Mrs. Winters, did you know that for only $29.95 you can buy Magic Wrinkle-No-More Cream from the TV?" I asked her.

Her face went as white as vanilla ice cream and her wrinkles slid right off her face as her mouth dropped open.

Wow! Just mentioning the Magic Wrinkle-No-More Cream made her wrinkles disappear! I was sure that cream had Magical Super Powers.

"And, Mrs. Winters," I continued, "It guarantees to make you look ten years younger!"

That's when her wrinkles came back, and her face went red, and her voice got all quivery.

"Connor, I think it may be best if you take a break with Mr. Hoover. I'll buzz him once I get back to the classroom and let him know you are on your way," Mrs. Winters said quietly.

"But, but . . . we have math!" I said.

All my bounciness slipped down my legs and into my feet. Then it shot right out of my toes at the thought of missing math class.

"Connor, we'll get to math afterward, I promise, but now you need to see Mr. Hoover," she said so quietly and even more slowly that I knew it was best not to argue.

Mrs. Winters looked like she had more wrinkles than ever and with all those extra wrinkles she looked about a hundred years old now!

I guess only super heroes have Magical Super Powers. How disappointing.

That is when I was 100 percent sure that today was definitely turning into a Very Discouraging Day.

I sure had a lot to explain to Mrs. Rosetti.

At least I only had 49 minutes left to wait.

Lesson 9

Mrs. Rosetti Has the Best Smiley Face

(Everyone needs someone to talk to)

I know there are 331 beige floor tiles from our classroom to the music room and 467 tiles to the gym. I'd never counted the tiles to Mr. Hoover's office before. Since I wasn't in any rush to see Ms. Robinson's nails again, I decided this was the perfect day to count them. There were 688 tiles! That was the highest count yet and an even number. Counting the tiles always gives me an awesome warm feeling in my stomach.

Mrs. Rosetti was standing in Mr. Hoover's doorway talking with him when I finally got there. Mrs. Rosetti looked over to me and smiled. Whenever she smiled it went all across her face and into the little crinkles around her olive-colored eyes.

"Mrs. Rosetti!" I said.

Her name came out of my mouth in a rush. It felt like I had been holding my breath for days. What a relief to see her. I could feel my legs get a bit of their bounce back as I rushed toward her.

"Hi, Connor, I'm so happy to see you," Mrs. Rosetti said.

I waved at her with both hands like I always do. I strongly dislike hugs and I have found that people won't try to hug you with your arms sticking straight out in front of you. They especially won't hug you when you wave your hands at them at the same time. My mom says that people will think you are still being friendly if you wave, because apparently, just sticking your arms straight out confuses most people.

"Mr. Hoover asked me to meet with you earlier than our regular time today, so let's head down to my room," Mrs. Rosetti explained.

Mr. Hoover handed her some sheets of paper and I spotted my name written on it.

"See you later, Connor," said

Connor Behavior
Report #57

-acting up in gym
class
-library stool mishap
-Spaghetti incident
-Chipped nails
issue
- rude comment
to Mrs. Winters

Mr. Hoover as he ruffled my hair.

I strongly dislike it when people mess up my hair, so it was very hard for me not to bat his hand away. I remembered that it was very, very Bad Manners to hit your principal, so I clenched my hands into tight fists, so they wouldn't fly out at Mr. Hoover.

"See you," I said.

I flattened down my hair, carefully smoothing my bangs back into place. In 62 tiles we were at Mrs. Rosetti's door.

"In you go, Connor," said Mrs. Rosetti. "I'm eager to hear about your day."

I sat in my most favorite chair in the entire

school. It's a moss-green vinyl recliner chair and it has no rips, snags, or marks anywhere on it.

Mrs. Rossetti sat in her gray swivel chair and dug out my file from the pile on her desk. She placed the papers from Mr. Hoover right on top and put them on her lap.

"Connor, tell me about your day," she said.

Mrs. Rosetti asks me this every day. One is a really bad day and five is the best day ever. Sometimes it's easy for me to figure out what number my day is and sometimes it's hard. Today I needed to think about my answer for a while.

"Well, Mrs. Rosetti, I thought it was going to be a really good day, maybe even a four. It started off really well, and then it got pretty bumpy and things just kept going wrong and now the day is not going well at all. I think it might be close to a two," I said.

"Connor, everyone has bumpy two-days, even me. I think it's great that you understand that the day is going a bit downhill, and together we'll try to find out why," said Mrs. Rosetti.

When Mrs. Rosetti said that, I felt my shoulders slide back toward my chair. Another big breath whooshed out of my mouth. It felt like my bones had gone all soft and all the jitters in my arms and legs disappeared.

"Thanks," I said.

"Tell me about gym class and library," said Mrs. Rosetti.

I told her all about Evan and how I couldn't understand why he didn't know what I was doing with the pins. I thought it would make a cartoon sound when the bowling pin hit his head. I never thought it would hurt him.

"Connor can you tell me why you hit Evan?" she asked.

"It was because he yelled in my ear," I said.

"I'm sure that didn't feel very nice, but you know it's not okay to hit. Is there something else you could have done?"

I stopped to think about that. Mrs. Rosetti is always telling me to slow down and try not to blurt out answers without giving my brain time to think. That's how the best answer came to me.

"I should have taken three deep breaths."

Mrs. Rosetti says taking those breaths will give my body time to calm down and then my brain gets more oxygen so I can make better choices. She taught me that the first time I met her in September and lots of times it really works. When I take a second for those deep breaths, it makes that tight feeling in my body soften up and my heart stops beating so fast. Sometimes my heart pounds so hard it feels like it's going to burst right out of my chest. True story.

Then I told her about the library and finding the Newest Best Book in the Universe and that it was too high to reach. Lastly, I shared my concerns about Jane's misunderstandings about stools and chairs.

I was pretty sure she would want to talk to Jane right away, but when I looked up at Mrs. Rosetti, her face wasn't smiley anymore. She had her Serious-No-Joking eyebrows on now. They looked like someone had drawn them on with a thin black marker and they pointed down toward her nose.

I felt a wave of heat spread up my neck, across my cheeks, and burn over my ears. I looked down to my lap where I made my hands do the "this is the church, and this is the steeple, open up the doors, and look at all the people."

"Connor, what are you feeling?" Mrs. Rosetti asked me quietly.

All sorts of thoughts swirled around in my head and it was really hard to focus on just one. I closed my eyes and one thought flew to the front of my brain and it said, *Take those three breaths!*

Lesson 10

Feelings Are Confusing

(Eyebrows can tell you a lot about a person)

"I think I am feeling embarrassed . . . and . . . sorry. I didn't mean to hurt Evan, Mrs. Rosetti. I know I shouldn't have hit him." I took another big gulp of air and whispered, "I'm just so tired of always getting things wrong. I'm tired of getting in trouble."

I looked straight out Mrs. Rosetti's window so I wouldn't have to look at her. I was sure she was going to be mad at me and never want to talk to me again.

"Connor, I am so proud of you," Mrs. Rosetti said.

Her voice sounded like my dad's when he sees my math tests. It sounds like laughing and crying all mixed up together.

I let just my left eye glance over to her and spied her smiley face. My heart flip-flopped. Phew! Her eyebrows were back to normal.

"You are getting so much better at taking responsibility for your actions and you are starting to recognize the feelings you're having," she said.

"Now, can you tell me

why you pushed Jane off a stool?" Mrs. Rosetti asked.

"I needed the stool to get the new *More All About Dogs* book . . . and Jane should've been sitting on a chair, not a stool," I said.

"So, you pushed her to the floor," said Mrs. Rosetti.

"Yeah, I guess," I said.

I really needed that book. Why couldn't anyone understand that?

"Was seeing that book the most exciting thing that happened to you

today?" she asked.

"Yeah," I said.

"Could there have been another way to get that book?" she asked.

"But I needed it right away!" I replied and then I noticed Mrs. Rosetti's eyebrows.

One eyebrow was pointing up to the ceiling and her other one was starting to do her Serious-No-Joking pointy straight black marker. So, I thought about it some more.

"Maybe, I could have taken three deep breaths, and then I guess I could have looked for the other stool or asked Mr. Cohen for help," I said.

Mrs. Rosetti's eyebrows slid back to their

normal place on her face and her eyes turned smiley again. I suppose that getting a different stool would have been easier, but I'm still surprised that Mrs. Rosetti was not concerned about Jane's own problem with stools.

"Lastly for today, Connor, can you tell me why you dumped spaghetti on your head?" Mrs. Rosetti said.

I took a deep gulp of air. This one was even hard for me to figure out.

"Mackenzie and I were having fun slurping up our spaghetti, especially when it got all sloppy down our chins. Everyone started laughing and next thing I knew, I was a caveman," I explained.

"And that is when you dumped spaghetti over your head?" asked Mrs. Rosetti.

"Yup," I replied. "And then I said 'Ooga Booga' because that's what cavemen say in cartoons."

"Is that when the kids laughed?" she asked.

"Yup, pretty much." I said.

"What did it feel like to have everyone laughing at something you did?" she asked.

"I don't know. I guess it felt . . . kind of . . . awesome. Everyone was looking at me and laughing and I had all their attention. It felt like I had lots of friends. It's weird. I felt like I was doing something right, because everyone was laughing . . . but at the same time I was doing something really wrong," I said.

"Well, it was pretty wrong to dump spaghetti over your head," agreed Mrs. Rosetti with a laugh. "What if you could find a way to get that

attention and get that same awesome feeling by doing something that was really right? What would that feel like, do you think?"

"That would be totally awesome!" I said.

I was feeling all bouncy in my chair and started tapping my feet against the foot rest of the recliner.

"I have some homework for you, and it's not like normal homework. I want you to figure out what is so special about you that no one else knows. I want you to think about something that you could share, show, or explain to your class that they would think was totally awesome," she said.

"I know a lot about dogs, math, and dinosaurs,

but everyone already knows that about me," I said.

"Hmmm," said Mrs. Rosetti. "It sounds like you've got some good ideas already."

She gave me the double thumbs up sign.

"I know you can figure this puzzle out, Connor. You'll find a way to make one of your favorite topics sound amazing for your class," she said as she stood up.

"We're out of time today, Connor, so we'll have to talk about Mrs. Winters and that face cream tomorrow. All the kids are already in the gym for the assembly."

"See you tomorrow, Mrs. Rosetti," I said and

did my straight-armed wave.

"Now go straight to the gym, Connor. No dilly-dallying," she said.

I started counting tiles on my way to the gym and was up to 54 when I reached the washroom. I was pretty sure that going to the bathroom wasn't dilly-dallying, and I really needed some quiet time to think.

Lesson 11

Not All People are Dog People

(Rotten bananas and fish
are never a good idea)

I was washing my hands when I heard heavy thumping race down the hallway. Then when I was drying my hands on my jeans I heard the custodian Mr. Marlin's Extended Keys jangling as he ran by the bathroom.

"I think he went back toward the library!" Mr. Marlin shouted.

No one answered Mr. Marlin, so I figured he was talking on his walkie-talkie. I was counting the floor tiles around the sink when Mr. Hoover's voice boomed out over the intercom.

"All teachers please follow a code yellow. Mr. O'Brien, please close the gymnasium doors. Any children not in the gym, please stay where you are and Mr. Marlin and I will come and get you."

A code yellow is serious business at Robert H. Crane School. It means we need to stay still and quiet in our classrooms until the principal

tells us the coast is clear! I figured it wouldn't hurt to poke my head out of the bathroom just a little bit. I'd take a quick look down the hallway and then pop my head right back inside.

"Whoa!" I whispered when I saw Mr. Marlin at the far end of the hall.

An enormous dirty yellow dog had Mr. Marlin pinned up against the wall with both its front paws. The dog was licking Mr. Marlin's face and its long straggly tail was wagging so fast it looked like a windmill.

The dog had clumps of mud mashed into its fur and I could see leaves and small twigs sticking out of its coat. That poor dog! No one had brushed it in a very long time.

Mr. Marlin's face was redder than my dad's

back when he got burnt on the beach last summer. Mr. Marlin's eyes were scrunched up tight and I could see his mouth moving but I couldn't hear what he was saying. So, I crept down the hall until I could hear.

"Nice doggy . . . please don't hurt me! Nice . . . doggy . . . help!" he gasped.

I sprinted down the rest of the hallway and stopped a few feet away from Mr. Marlin and the dog. Peeuw! What a stench! From this close I could smell a disgusting mix of fish and rotten bananas. I guessed no one had bathed it in a very long time, either. The dog looked a lot like either a Golden Retriever or a Nova Scotia Duck Toller.

It had a mud covered blue collar and dog tags poking out of the matted fur around its neck. If this dog had a collar and tags, then I figured it had to belong to someone. It must have gotten lost. That's when I knew I had to help that dog. I sat down on the floor.

"Here, boy . . . here, boy," I called and clapped my hands.

It immediately stopped slurping Mr. Marlin's face and slid down Mr. Marlin's stomach to the ground. The dog swung its head toward me—and it smiled!

"Rrummph," it snort-barked.

It looked a lot like Charlie, but that seemed

impossible.

I clapped my hands again and then patted my lap. Could this really be Charlie?

"Here, boy!" I called.

The dog bounded over to me and leaped into my lap. It was so heavy that it knocked me over, sat on my chest, and barked into my face.

Its dirty dog tag dangled over my nose and swayed back and forth. I reached up to the tag with one hand and gently stroked the fur at the back of its neck with my other.

"Connor! Oh, no! Connor!" I could hear Mr. Marlin yelling.

"Shhh, boy. It's okay, you're safe," I whispered

to the dog.

"C-H-A-R-L-I-E," I read as I scraped his tag clean.

"It is you!" I cried.

He was so far from home! I hugged him with all my might and he licked my face with all his might. Ick. Charlie had never smelled rotten before.

"Connor! Connor!" Mr. Marlin shouted.

I peered over Charlie's shoulder to where Mr. Marlin had been squashed against the wall. Mr. Marlin was now standing on a large overturned garbage can with his long black flashlight in his hand. He always carried it on a hook around his waist next to his Extended Keys and his walkie-talkie. Mr. Marlin said he lived by the Boy Scout

motto, "Always be prepared."

"The dog's got him! THE DOG HAS GOT HIM!"

Mr. Marlin yelled into his walkie-talkie.

Mr. Marlin was shaking from head to toe and

was panting harder than Charlie. I pushed Charlie off me and stood up.

"Mr. Marlin, I'm okay! Charlie was just happy to see me. He's very friendly and licking me is just his way of saying 'hi'," I said.

"Rrrough!" said Charlie.

Mr. Marlin's eyes rolled closed, his knees buckled, and he slid down the wall. I think he fainted.

I guess no one had taught him to take three deep breaths.

That's when Mr. Hoover came barreling around the corner with a broom in his hand.

Lesson 12

A Code Yellow Is Serious Business

(Dogs have an excellent sense of direction)

"Sit, Charlie. Stay, boy," I said and held my hand flat in front of his face.

That's dog sign language for "Don't move."

I began petting Charlie's head to show Mr. Hoover how gentle Charlie was.

Mr. Hoover looked from me to Charlie to Mr. Marlin and then back to me again. Mr. Marlin's eyes started to blink open.

"That dog attacked me!" Mr. Marlin gasped.

His face flushed red all at once.

"Connor," Mr. Hoover said quietly, "slowly back away from that dog. We've called animal control and they're sending out a crew to catch him."

"Animal control! But Mr. Hoover, this is Charlie! I know this dog. You don't have to be scared," I explained.

Then I got an Excellent Idea.

"Watch this!" I said.

"Shake a paw, Charlie," I said and he lifted one grubby paw.

"Roll over, Charlie."

He rolled over and I could see thick mud all over his belly.

"Dance, Charlie."

He sat on his hind legs and reached his front paws up toward me. I took his paws and we danced in a tiny circle in the hallway. Charlie's fishy smell made my stomach flip over, so I had to turn my head to gulp in fresh air as we twirled.

"Now bow, Charlie."

He sat down and then slid one leg straight out in front of him and bowed his head. Just like I had taught him.

"Good boy, Charlie!" I said and ruffled the dirty fur around his collar.

He always liked pats there best.

"Well done, Connor . . . and Charlie!" Mrs. Rosetti said.

I was so busy showing off Charlie's tricks for Mr. Marlin and Mr. Hoover that I didn't notice that Mrs. Rosetti had snuck up behind me.

I spun around and pointed to Charlie.

"It's Charlie, Mrs. Rosetti! This is the dog I was always telling you about!" I said. "Remember? I told you that Bonnie just moved away and how much I missed Charlie? And remember I told you that Charlie ran away? I guess Charlie wanted to come back to his old home and here he is!"

"I think Charlie wanted to come back to see you and here he is," said Mrs. Rosetti.

"I told Mr. Marlin he didn't need to be scared," I explained to Mrs. Rosetti.

"I wasn't scared," said Mr. Marlin, ". . . not exactly."

"We can call off animal control, thanks to Connor," said Mr. Hoover as he ruffled my hair. "Mr. Marlin, would you please head to the gym and let them know what's happened?"

I was so happy to see Charlie that I didn't even mind my hair being messed up.

"Mr. Hoover, can I speak with you for a

moment?" asked Mrs. Rosetti.

Mrs. Rosetti winked at me and they walked far down the hallway talking in whispers.

I bent over Charlie and carefully began pulling the twigs and leaves out of his fur. He looked up at me and smiled his toothy smile. Then he licked me right up my nose. Yick. He really needed a bath—and his teeth brushed.

"Connor," called Mrs. Rosetti, "could you and Charlie please come here?"

"Come, Charlie," I said and slapped my thigh.

Charlie walked right at my side looking up at me and panting. His tongue hung out the side of his mouth.

"Connor, I think you've already completed the homework I gave you. Faster than I ever expected, too," said Mrs. Rosetti.

"I did?" I asked.

I was confused. All I had figured out was that I wanted to show my class how incredible dogs were. But I still had not figured out *how* I was going to do that.

"Connor, you just showed Mr. Marlin, Mr. Hoover, and me exactly how much you know about dogs. You also showed us all the great tricks that you can do with Charlie. We had a code yellow in our school and thanks to you and everything you know about dogs . . . you saved the day! I would say if you put all those things together, your class would think that you and Charlie are totally awesome!" said Mrs. Rosetti.

"So," said Mr. Hoover, "do you think you and Charlie would like to show off your tricks to the rest of the kids right now? Afterward, we'll call Bonnie to come and pick up Charlie."

"Sure! But everyone is in the gym for an assembly," I said.

"How do you feel about a bigger audience than just your class, Connor?" asked Mrs. Rosetti.

"You mean the whole school?" I asked.

Whoa. Butterflies flew around my stomach and then zoomed down my legs and arms.

"That's right, the whole school. Are you up for it?" asked Mrs. Rosetti.

She kneeled down in front of me and smoothed my hair into place. I could feel my butterflies start to settle down as she gently stroked my hair.

"That would be *way* better than being a caveman eating spaghetti," I said.

Lesson 13

Stomach Swirls Can Be Both Good and Bad at the Same Time

(Good dental hygiene is important for humans and dogs)

When Mrs. Rosetti, Charlie, and I walked into the gym, the entire school was already there and they were all looking at us. It was like we were rock stars. All the kids and the teachers started clapping and cheering. Some of the sixth graders even stomped their feet on the floor and whistled with their fingers. My stomach started whirling around and it felt weird. It was both a good whirling and a bad whirling at the same time. Charlie shied up next to me, but his tail was still wagging, only slower than usual. I think Charlie must have been having stomach whirls too.

Mr. Hoover zipped around us to the podium at the front of the gym.

"Okay, kids . . . settle down now. Settle down," he said.

It took another minute or two but the teachers were able to get the kids to be quiet.

"As you know, we had a code yellow in the school and I wanted to thank you all for following our rules so well. As you also know by now, we had an intruder in the school, and it wasn't quite

what anyone had

ever expected!" said

Mr. Hoover and he laughed.

He pointed over to me and Charlie and all the

kids started cheering again. Mrs. Rosetti then

walked up to the podium and started speaking.

"Well, thanks to Connor Campbell in room P3, we are all safe from this friendly, but rather dirty, dog named Charlie. Connor was able to calm him down and control him, because Connor is an expert on dogs and Connor knows Charlie really well," said Mrs. Rosetti. "Connor has spent a lot of time training Charlie and we thought it would be fun for everyone at Robert H. Crane to see what Connor can do with Charlie."

Mrs. Rosetti looked right at me and started clapping. That got all the kids clapping again and my stomach started whirling again.

I took a few slow steps toward her, but my hands got so sweaty I had to stop and wipe them on my shorts.

Mrs. Rosetti hurried over and knelt down in front of me, right next to Charlie.

"Connor, what are you thinking?" she asked.

"That I might actually throw up, but I don't want to be sick, because I'm not doing one of my experiments right now. And I think it would be embarrassing to throw up in front of the entire school," I said quietly so no one but Mrs. Rosetti would hear.

Then I closed my eyes and took one deep breath and let it whoosh out of my mouth. My breath must have blown right into Mrs. Rosetti's face, but I couldn't be sure because my eyes were

scrunched closed so I could concentrate on my breathing. I hoped my breath wasn't too stinky. At least it wouldn't smell like rotten bananas and fish like Charlie's. Then I took two more giant breaths and guess what? I could feel the whirls start to melt away in my stomach.

That's when I opened my eyes and Charlie pushed in between us and licked me up my nose again. Peuww! Mrs. Rosetti was definitely luckier than me!

Lesson 14

Kids Love Dog Tricks

(Feeling like the king of the school is . . . totally awesome!)

"Charlie, come," I commanded, and we marched right up next to the podium at the front of the gym.

I looked out at all the kids sitting there and felt a rush of warmth whoosh up my back. It wasn't a red-fire-hotness, like when I nudged Jane off of the stool, but a nice calming feeling. It made me smile. I took one more deep breath and began.

"Charlie is a Golden Retriever. Goldens are

one of the top five most popular breeds of dogs. They are eager to be your friend and are gentle, playful, and loyal. When compared to other dogs, they are very fast learners, which means they do very well in obedience training. It's important that they are trained really well because they are big and strong and they want a lot of attention," I explained. "If you don't train them well they are like an out of control toddler and when you're not looking they can eat things like shoes, backpacks, and even furniture."

"Now I would like to show you Charlie's tricks," I said.

The kids cheered again.

I started with the easy ones, like sit, rollover and shake a paw. Then I had Charlie do his bow and we danced.

The kids loved Charlie and I had the best tingly feeling zooming through my whole body!

So how did my day go? Well it sure had some bumps and the spaghetti on my head was pretty bad, but I think it had a totally awesome ending.

I'm looking forward to tomorrow. We're going on a field trip to the Manitoba Museum and they have a new exhibit. They have life-sized model

dinosaurs, a dinosaur movie, and a fossil sand box where you can dig for dinosaur bones.

I can hardly wait to tell Mrs. Winters all about the differences between the Tyrannosaurus Rex and the Giganotosaurus. I'll have to remember to bring my *Dinosaur Digest* book with me. Mrs. Winters will love to hear all those facts!

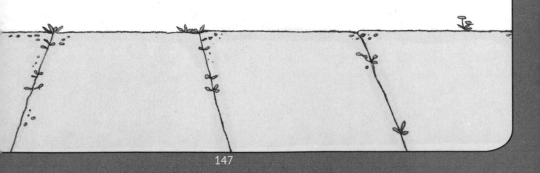

The End

Our Mission

Little Pickle Press is dedicated to helping parents and educators cultivate conscious, responsible little people by stimulating explorations of the meaningful topics of their generation through a variety of media, technologies, and techniques.

Little Pickle Press
Environmental Benefits Statement

book is printed on BPM Inc. Envirographic™ 100 paper. Made in the USA, it is
recipient of the Governor's Award of Excellence in Energy Efficiency. It is made
100% PCRF (Post-Consumer Recovered Fiber) collected in North America. It is
®-certified, acid-free, and 100% Process Chlorine-Free Certified.

e Pickle Press saved the following resources by using Envirographic™ 100 paper:

trees	energy	greenhouse gases	wastewater	solid waste
st-consumer covered fiber places wood er with savings anslated as es.	PCRF content displaces energy used to process equivalent virgin fiber.	Measured in CO_2 equivalents, PCRF content and Green Power reduce greenhouse gas emissions.	PCRF content eliminates wastewater needed to process equivalent virgin fiber.	PCRF content eliminates solid waste generated by producing an equivalent amount of virgin fiber through the pulp and paper manufacturing process.
46 trees	21 mil BTUs	4,007 lbs	21,736 gal	1,455 lbs

Calculations based on research by the Environmental Paper Network's Paper Calculator.

*e print and distribute our materials in an environmentally-friendly
manner, using recycled paper, soy inks, and green packaging.*

About The Author

Jodi Carmichael is an author, speaker, day-dreamer, and an advocate for Asperger Manitoba Inc. Jodi lives in Winnipeg, Manitoba with her two wildly imaginative daughters, patient and supportive husband, and Border Terrier named Zoe.
Visit Jodi on the web at www.jodicarmichael.com.

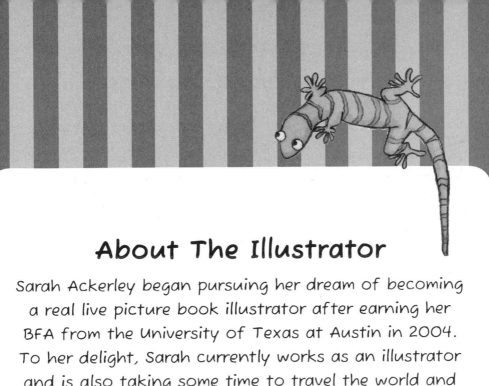

About The Illustrator

Sarah Ackerley began pursuing her dream of becoming a real live picture book illustrator after earning her BFA from the University of Texas at Austin in 2004. To her delight, Sarah currently works as an illustrator and is also taking some time to travel the world and paint murals wherever she finds a needy wall.

Visit Sarah on the web at www.sarahackerley.com.

Other Award-Winning Books from Little Pickle Press

BIG
Written by Coleen Paratore
Illustrated by Clare Fennell

Ripple's Effect
Written by Shawn Achor and Amy Blankson
Illustrated by Cecilia Rebora

Snutt the Ift
Written and Illustrated by Helen Ward

Your Fantastic Elastic Brain
Written by JoAnn Deak, Ph.D.
Illustrated by Sarah Ackerley

Sofia's Dream
Written by Land Wilson
Illustrated by Sue Cornelison

What Does It Mean To Be Safe?
Written by Rana DiOrio
Illustrated by Sandra Salsbury

What Does It Mean To Be Present?
Written by Rana DiOrio
Illustrated by Eliza Wheeler

What Does It Mean To Be Green?
Written by Rana DiOrio
Illustrated by Chris Blair

What Does It Mean To Be Global?
Written by Rana DiOrio
Illustrated by Chris Hill

www.littlepicklepress.com